Published by Hodder Children's Books 2001

Design by Fiona Webb

10 9 8 7 6 5 4 3 2 1

ISBN: 0 340 787767

Printed by The Guernsey Press Co Ltd, Guernsey, Channel Islands

Hodder Children's Books
a division of Hodder Headline Limited
338 Euston Road
London NW1 3BH

STRESS

Anita Naik

Illustrated by Jennifer Graham

Hodder

Contents

Other essential

BULLYING
Michele Elliott

DIVORCE AND SEPARATION
Matthew Whyman

DRUGS
Anita Naik

EATING
Anita Naik

PERIODS
Charlotte Owen

SELF ESTEEM
Anita Naik

SEX
Anita Naik

SMOKING
Matthew Whyman

SPOTS
Anita Naik

YOUR RIGHTS
Anita Naik

Introduction

We all get stressed out over life. Maybe you feel it when you argue with your family, or when you fall in and out of love. Perhaps it gets to you most when exams are looming or just before the results come out. You may even experience stress when you're just waiting for a bus or queuing up in a shop.

The fact is stress is a normal and natural part of life. Try to get rid of it completely and your life will become boring. On the other hand, if you have too much of it, your health and happiness will start to suffer. Stress over-load happens to everyone at times, and the answer is not to bury your head under a pillow, or to work harder and faster. The key is to face it head on and deal with the parts you really can't cope with.

Easier said than done, of course, which is why I've put together this book on stress just for you. Apart from looking at all the areas that can cause you stress in your life (peers, school-work, your body and family), it also explains how stress can make you feel and act.

Work your way through this book and you'll find some helpful and easy techniques to take the pressure off. Are you ready to de-stress?

Anita

CHAPTER ONE

What is stress?

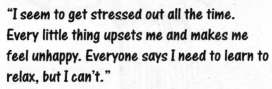

"I seem to get stressed out all the time.
Every little thing upsets me and makes me
feel unhappy. Everyone says I need to learn to
relax, but I can't."

Tanya (13)

"Sometimes I find myself screaming and
shouting at my parents, but I don't know why."

Toni (13)

Stress is ... anxiety, pressure, tension, strain, worry, dread, fear. Stress causes ... illness, depression, unhappiness, and distress. Stress affects ... everyone!

Little wonder then, that there are about a million books out there dedicated to helping people de-stress, calm down and chill out. This one is different because it is aimed specifically at you and the stress which affects your world.

It's likely you've heard the word 'stress' thrown about by everyone, from your parents and teachers to your friends and their friends. Most people blame it for their bad moods, their tiredness, their irritability and their lack of time.

If this sounds familiar, it might surprise you to know that stress in itself isn't a bad thing. After all, it's the force that gets us going, makes us want to try, gets us out of tricky situations and helps us to recognise when we're in danger. It's only when stress levels rise above normal and you feel you just can't cope anymore that you need to do something … and fast.

WHERE DOES STRESS COME FROM?

Stress is linked to our most basic human response – the 'fight or flight' instinct. This goes back zillions of years to when primitive people were caught daily in physically threatening situations. When faced, say with a sabre-toothed tiger, the body would release stress chemicals (adrenaline) which would cause the heart to beat faster, blood pressure to rise, muscles to tense up and the brain to become alert, ready to either run ('flight') or stay ('fight').

Either way, the physical activity used up the extra adrenaline in the body. These days we rarely have a physical response to stress because it is usually emotional not physical in nature, e.g. fear of failing. Therefore the adrenaline levels stay high and our bodies remain in a state of constant over-alertness which leads to high levels of anxiety.

WHAT CAN MAKE YOU STRESSED?

The funny thing about stress is that everything, even good things, can make you stressed and anxious. Think of when you have a party, or go on a school holiday. You're happy, but you're also tense and probably a little worried about the situation. While this kind of stress can make you feel uncomfortable and anxious, it's not as painful or as consuming as the stress which comes from more traumatic situations.

Below is a list of the top ten causes of teenage stress:

1. Death of a loved one
2. Divorce in the family
3. Personal injury or illness
4. Relationships
5. Friendships
6. Start or end of school/exams
7. Change in living conditions
8. Changing schools
9. Christmas and holidays
10. Minor law violation

This list shows we can't always be responsible for what's causing us stress. Perhaps you have a father or mother with a drink problem or parents who fight all the time. Maybe your family has job or money worries that make you feel scared about the future. Perhaps there is pressure coming from outside the home – you may be worried about the future or feel that you can't handle your exams. You could be unhappy about being single and on your own. All these things add up to one thing ... STRESS OVERLOAD.

However, the good news is that, while we can't always control the causes of our stress, we can be responsible for how we deal with them. Handle them in the right way and you'll defuse a potentially stressful situation and ease the pressure off. But it's all too easy to get into a stress spiral.

Here's an example: your mum is having a bad day and forgets she said your friends could come over. Instead of reminding her gently, you fly off the handle, over-react and cry. This leads her to retaliate because you're making her stress levels worse, and in turn this makes you even more stressed.

HOW STRESS CAN MAKE YOU FEEL

When you get over-stressed, you may start to notice some changes in your body:

- tiredness
- tearfulness
- unhappiness
- anxiety
- misery

- anger
- depression
- irritation
- fearfulness

If these sound familiar, don't worry. Contrary to popular belief, such things aren't imaginary – they happen to most people, whatever their age.

If your stress levels are high, you could find yourself suffering from the following common responses:

1. Headaches and migraines

"I suffer from really terrible headaches. They usually happen when I'm at school and when I'm studying for exams. I had my eyes checked out because I thought I needed glasses but I didn't. So what's wrong with me?"

Sarah (14)

Most headaches are triggered by muscular tension. They occur because stress and anxiety causes tension in the muscles around your shoulders and neck, thereby, causing a headache. Some people describe tension headaches as a tight elastic band around the head, a pain above the eyes and an ache in the neck. Though pain relievers can help, changing your lifestyle is a more permanent way to deal with these headaches. For starters, make sure you have a regular sleep pattern, don't skip meals, take up physical exercise and eat healthily.

If you suffer from regular tension headaches, see your doctor, as he or she can usually give you something to help in the short term. For longer-term results you need to get to the bottom of what's stressing you out.

"Now and again I have a terrible headache that lasts for hours. I don't usually suffer from headaches but this one is terrible. I have to lie down and shut the curtains until it goes away. It also makes me feel sick and my eyesight goes funny. I worry that I have a brain tumour."

Toni (13)

Toni suffers from what is known as a migraine. It is thought that migraines are caused by temporary changes to the blood vessels around the brain. It is still not known why these changes take place but stress is often a major factor.

Migraines are pounding headaches (usually on one side of the head) that can last for hours or even days. They are accompanied by distorted eyesight, feelings of nausea and sometimes even vomiting. Once the headache stage of an attack starts, most people cannot bear bright lights or noise and have to lie in a darkened room.

There is no cure for migraines but there are lots of things you can do to avoid them and help alleviate the symptoms. First, seeing your doctor. He or she can help find the right treatment to combat your condition. Apart from drug treatments, relaxation and finding your particular 'trigger' (the object, situation or stress that causes the attack to come on) can help. Some foods are known as migraine triggers: cheese, chocolate and oranges. Lack of food and changes to your sleeping patterns are also common culprits. Some people find that when they avoid triggers they don't get migraines. Keep a diary to try to help you identify your personal triggers.

2. Panic attacks

"Sometimes I feel like I just can't breathe. I'll be doing something normal like sitting with my friends eating lunch and the room will start to spin. Then my heart will start beating really fast and I'll feel cold and sweaty. My teacher thinks it's a panic attack. But I don't understand, it never seems to happen when I'm in a stressful situation."

Heather (14)

Panic attacks like Heather's are extremely frightening. They seem to come out of the blue and not necessarily at a time when you feel in a panic. And the huge range of physical symptoms are so scary and distressing that sufferers often feel as if they are going to die. The good news is these attacks do not lead to death or serious illness.

However, you may experience one or a few of the following:

- Palpitations (abnormal heart-beat).
- Your breath catches in your throat.
- Your chest may tighten.
- You may start to hyperventilate (very rapid or deep breathing causing dizziness, fainting, etc.).
- You imagine you're going to collapse.
- You wonder if you're having a heart attack.
- You get sweaty and cold.
- You might feel claustrophobic (abnormal fear of being in an enclosed space).
- You might feel nauseous and dizzy.
- You may hear a ringing in your ear.
- You may feel an overwhelming sense of doom and terror.
- Your nerves may feel on edge.

Under normal circumstances, when something stressful happens, your mind reacts as if you are under threat. This causes your body to gear up for the 'fight or flight' response (see page3). Usually, stress levels then go back to normal as your body recognises you are not really under attack, or the threat has passed.

However, if your stress remains high and you start living with a lot of anxiety and tension in your life, your body will stay on red alert all the time. This means that every time you're in a stressful situation your stress levels will immediately get too high, your body will exaggerate its response and you'll be more likely to have a panic attack.

If your attacks have begun recently and you can't work out why you're under so much stress, it might help to know that it takes just one painful or highly stressful situation to trigger an attack. For instance:

- A parents' divorce.
- A death in the family.
- The break-up of a relationship.
- Failing an exam.
- Your own or someone else's illness.
- An accident.

Experts have also found the following types of people are the ones most likely to suffer from panic attacks:

- People who can't relax.
- People who are usually very self-critical.
- People who have high expectations of themselves.
- Perfectionists.

If this sounds familiar, it's also worth noting that the kind of lifestyle you lead can make you prone to panic attacks. If you want to check whether you're under too much anxiety, ask yourself the following:

- Are you overcome with the pressures of juggling your school life and home life?
- Do you find relationships and friendships a strain?
- Do you eat badly?
- Do you rob yourself of a good night's sleep?
- Do you criticize yourself for not being a better person?
- Do you constantly tell yourself you 'must' do this?
- Do you have a list of 'aims' in your life?
- Do you bottle up your feelings?
- Do you constantly worry without being able to reach a solution?

If you answer 'yes' to any of these questions, it's important to be aware of what you're doing to yourself. It's these very attitudes that can weaken your ability to cope with ordinary life and give you a lot of internal stress.

ZAPPING THE STRESS OF PANIC ATTACKS

The way to conquer your panic attacks is to acknowledge you have the power to control your panic. Remember, you do not have to live with panic attacks for life. You can get over them by following this advice:

1 Try cupping your hands or holding a paper bag over your nose and mouth, and breathing into it for 10 minutes. This will raise levels of carbon dioxide in the bloodstream, steady your breathing and relieve your symptoms.
2 Don't suffer in silence. Tell your friends, family or teachers what is happening and how they can

help. Remember, panic attacks are nothing to be ashamed of.

3 Reduce the power of the panic attacks by reassuring yourself they won't harm you.

4 Realise you have control over your fears. Many people who have panic attacks have vivid imaginations which they use to conjure up disaster. Train your thoughts to focus on situations where you feel safe and secure – for example, watching a certain film with a particular person in your bedroom.

5 If you feel trapped and stuck, write down a list of what's making you feel this way. Then look at the list again and, with the help of someone your trust, work out what you can do to help yourself.

6 Consider seeing a counsellor or behavioural therapist. These experts can help you confront your fears and overcome your panic.

7 Learn to relax and let go of your stresses. Relaxation techniques such as learning to breathe easily can help release tension and help you to cope when you're having an attack.

8 See your doctor for advice about drugs he or she can offer you to alleviate the panic in the short term.

3. Self-harm

"Sometimes I just can't cope with things. I feel trapped and I find myself doing awful things. I usually use scissors on my arms and scratch at myself until I bleed. Afterwards I feel so ashamed."

Jill (13)

Self-harm is when someone injures themselves on purpose – for example, by scratching or cutting their skin. They use it as a coping mechanism for dealing with life's stresses and worries.

People who know nothing about self-harm view it as a form of attention-seeking, but doctors now view it as a way of expressing deep distress and frustration. Many young people find themselves under severe pressure from families, school, friends and boyfriends/girlfriends. Pressure, for example, to do well at school, be a 'good' daughter/son, or to fit in with your peers. These external pressures become internalised when people feel they have no one to confide in. The feeling of being powerless and worthless then translates into hurting themselves.

If you are harming yourself, you need to seek professional help. Your doctor can refer you to an experienced psychotherapist or counsellor who can help you to find new ways of coping and help you get to the root of your self-harm.

You can recover from self-harm once you learn to deal with the reasons underlying your actions. This process may be hard and painful, but with the right kind of professional help it is possible.

If you want to make a start on working out why you hurt yourself, ask yourself the following:

- When do you hurt yourself?
- How does hurting yourself help you to cope?

- Are there any situations that always cause you to injure yourself?
- How do you feel after you've hurt yourself?

By answering these questions you'll be able to make a start in understanding why you do the things you do. Remember, if you give yourself a severe cut you need to seek immediate medical attention.

HELPING SOMEONE WHO HURTS THEMSELVES

The first step in helping someone who self-injures is to realise that there is nothing 'crazy' or 'wrong' about someone who hurts themselves. As frightening as it is, you must try not to add to their stress.

The best way to help a friend who hurts themselves is to offer your support and understanding – but don't think you can change them. It's rather like dealing with someone with an addiction. Until they decide for themselves that they want to stop, they will not be able to do so.

This doesn't mean you have to keep quiet about how you feel. In fact, it can be good to let your friend know that their behaviour upsets you, but that you understand and want to help. Listening can help more than you think.

GET TO GRIPS

Of course, we all have different ways of dealing with what stresses us out and upsets us. Some of us shout and scream while others cry and hide away. Many try to shake it off by working incredibly hard or exercising to extremes. These are our own personal coping mechanisms – they may not work for anyone else. but up to a point they may work well for you.

But what happens when they don't work any more? Or when you can't sleep at night? What do you do when you feel like crying all the time? You may lock yourself away or pretend that it just isn't happening, and if you do either or both of those two things you'll know that it doesn't help. All it does is make the problem worse.

It's important to realise that stress overload of any kind has a lot to do with storing up your anxieties, fears and worries. Read on and learn how to get to grips with your everyday stresses such as peer pressure, school-work, your body and family. Learn exactly how stress works and why, and you'll be able to lower your stress levels for life.

CHAPTER TWO

Peer pressure

"I like being with my friends, but sometimes I feel like I am different from them. They talk about things that don't interest me; boys, sex, and bunking off school. My mum says I don't have to be like them, but it's hard not to. I don't want to be left out, or be seen as a loser."

Karen (14)

If you're best friends and you trust each other, how come being together stresses you out? How come your friend is telling you how to live your life? Is it that they just want the best for you, or do they have a different agenda? Here are some things good friends don't do:

- Stress their friends out over their personal choices.
- Pressurise their friends to do things they don't want to do.
- Make fun of you, when you decide to be different.
- Threaten to take their friendship away if you don't toe the line.
- Tell people your innermost secrets.

- Put you down and make you feel bad when you disagree.
- Make you think you're not good enough.
- Encourage you to lie, cheat, steal or bunk off school.

WHAT IS PEER PRESSURE?

Peer pressure is the stress you get from people your own age to act, think and look a certain way. Peer pressure is usually only associated with negative influences, but it actually affects everything from fashion and music, to boyfriends and the way you behave with others. In many ways, it's about conforming to and fitting in with your friends' lifestyles.

You may think you're not under any pressure, if so that's great, but be aware that peer pressure can come in a number of different forms. If your friends try to persuade, manipulate or even coerce you into things, they are applying peer pressure. Of course, not all peer pressure is bad. Knowing your friends would be upset and disappointed with you if you stole from them is a good pressure.

However, peer pressure is often negative, and if you're not careful you can find yourself in stressful and potentially risky situations. There are times when giving in to peer pressure can feel like the right thing to do. After all, why do you have to be in at 8pm when all your friends get to stay out until 10pm? And why can't you smoke when all your friends do?

As you can see, peer pressure comes in many different forms. In an ideal world I'd say, ignore peer pressure and be yourself, but let's face it, that's not always the most stress-free option.

HOW PEER PRESSURE CAN MAKE YOU FEEL

"My parents say, if your friends jumped off a cliff would you follow? Of course I wouldn't, but what comfort is that when I feel left out and dorky for not being allowed to stay out late with them?"

Paul (13)

"I smoke even though I know it's bad for me, and that my parents would kill me if they found out. I know it sounds stupid that I do it because all my friends do, but they'd think I was weird if I didn't."

Susie (14)

"My mum doesn't want me to go that far with the boys I am dating. I don't want to let her down, but it's so hard when all my friends seem to be having sex with their boyfriends. I worry about it all the time. It's tough trying to keep everyone happy."

Lisa (13)

Peer pressure can spark off some strong feelings ...

1. Loneliness

"Sometimes I am with my best friends and, suddenly, I feel very lonely. I don't understand it."

Amy (12)

Do you ever feel lonely in a crowd of your friends? That feeling where everyone is chatting and having a good time, and you feel completely out of place.

If you do, you're experiencing the stress of isolation. Feeling lonely amongst friends is about feeling they don't really know who you are. If your answer to the above question is 'yes', it's probably because you're trying too hard to be what everyone else wants you to be, and not being yourself.

Try asking yourself how well your friends know you?

- Can they list five good things about you without thinking too hard?
- Can they tell you what you love and what you hate?
- Can they say what scares you? Or what makes you cry?
- Would they be there for you in a crisis?

If your friends don't know you, it could be because you've not been 100% honest with them. If this is the case, ask yourself why? Are you afraid they won't like you? That somehow you won't meet their expectations? If so, remember this: true friends like you for who you are.

2. Fear and anxiety

> "There are days when I feel afraid that my friends don't like me. I keep thinking I must act happy, otherwise they won't want to be around me."
>
> **Jo (13)**

> "It's OK to say be yourself, but I know people will really hate me if they found out that I'm more into animals than going out and meeting boys. So I pretend it's naff to like animals."
>
> **Suzanne (13)**

Are you afraid to be yourself around your friends? Are you worried that they'll see your house, parents or car and suddenly decide you're not worth knowing any more? Are you worried that they'll make fun of you if they found out the 'truth' about what you really like to do away from them? If so, it's time to look at that 'truth' and what's really worrying you.

Plenty of people worry they are not good enough for their friends, and so put on an act for the people around them. They pretend they live a certain way, have a boyfriend, go on expensive holidays – anything to make their friends think they are as good as them.

It's completely normal to feel a certain amount of anxiety when you're meeting new people, or have seen someone you fancy. This type of anxiety is more about wanting to make a good impression, and goes once you begin to get to know someone. However, it's worth remembering that real friendships are about wanting to be with someone because you like them and for no other reason.

3. Embarrassment

"On Saturdays I have to go shopping with my mum in the supermarket and I hate it. I get really anxious that someone will see me and they'll think I'm a baby for having to do the shopping."

Chris (14)

There's one fact you have to always keep in mind – you're as good as you think you are! It's a waste of time getting stressed-out because you feel your parents aren't trendy or your mum works somewhere embarrassing.

At one point or another we all feel ashamed about an area in our life that we see as abnormal. This leads us to imagine that if our friends found out, they'd be horrified and ditch us immediately. The fact is everyone's lives are different and what is seen as

weird to one person is perfectly normal to another.
The world would be a boring place if we were all the
same.

4. Sadness

*"Sometimes I look at girls my own age and I feel
sad about my own life. I don't have very many
friends, I'm not popular and I don't have a
boyfriend. I know things would be better if I were
pretty or funny."*

Karen (14)

Do you feel sad because your friends all seem happy
and you're not? Sad because you haven't got a
boyfriend or any money? If you feel like this, it's likely
you're feeling stressed-out about your life because
you've concocted a list in your head of all the things
that would make you happy. Your list might include

things like a boyfriend, more money, better looks and a bigger house. Often wanting all these things can actually cause you stress and unhappiness. Ask yourself these questions: Are rich people all happy? Are beautiful people always full of joy? Of course not. Likewise, having a boyfriend doesn't solve your problems. It's easy to think these things would make your life easier, but the truth is they won't. Only you can take the stress off yourself and allow yourself to feel good.

The next time you feel any of the above, remind yourself of the following:

- Anxiety and fear has no place in a real friendship.
- True friends like you for yourself and nothing else.
- Now and then everyone feels anxious about not being good enough.
- A certain amount of stress is normal when you meet new people.
- You wouldn't be human if you didn't want your friends to like you.
- Friends who judge you on your clothes, house or way of life aren't 'true' friends.

WHAT TO DO WHEN YOUR FRIENDS AREN'T YOUR 'TRUE' FRIENDS

It's never easy when you discover your friends are really your enemies. If this happens then there is really only one thing you can do and that's walk away. It's impossible to change people who don't want to change, and therefore, all you can do is change the situation. This means taking yourself away from them. Easier said than done!

Here are some things you can do to help the situation:

1 Avoid a face-to-face confrontation about why you don't want to be friends.
2 Make the break short and to the point. Throwing recriminations will only make a bad situation worse.
3 Avoid your usual hangouts for a while, until it all blows over.
4 Be nice when you do meet, so they know there are no hard feelings.

PRESSURE FROM THE MEDIA

 Peer pressure is not the only influence on our life. Often the media – magazines, television or books – add to peer pressure. Here are some ways to combat a few of the most common pressures:

THE STRESS: "Everyone needs a boyfriend or girlfriend."

We are constantly being told by films, television and songs how great it is to be in love and because of this, most of us start to imagine we're failures if we're not in love.

This leads us to believe that if we're single there's something not quite right about ourselves. As if somehow, having a boyfriend or girlfriend actually makes us a better person and more attractive.

The stress of not being like everyone else can sometimes force us to conform and settle for something we're not happy with. That's why it's important to realise there is no reason to have a boyfriend/girlfriend unless you meet someone you really want to be with. What's wrong with being single? You have your freedom, independence, and a chance to find yourself.

If you're so desperate for a boyfriend or girlfriend that you just can't bear being single, then you need to ask yourself why? Are you hoping that a boyfriend or girlfriend will solve all the problems in your life? Do you think having one will make you less lonely? More attractive? Or more acceptable to your friends? If any of these are your reasons then you need to think again. Boyfriends or girlfriends are supposed to be a plus in life, not the whole reason for living.

DE-STRESS TIPS:

- Do everything you want to do with your life now, don't wait until you have a boyfriend or girlfriend.
- Refuse to let anyone make you feel bad for being single.
- Be pro-active; don't just complain that all your friends have partners – organise things, make arrangements, go out.

THE STRESS: "If you were cool you'd do this ... the pressure to drink or take drugs."

People use drink and drugs for all kinds of reasons. Some to feel better about themselves, some to escape from their lives, some to fit in with their friends and others because they just can't get through the day without them.

If you haven't yet been tempted to try any of these things, I'd like to say – 'Don't do it! They aren't worth bothering with.' However, we all know it's not that easy. Drink and drugs are tempting for a number of reasons, not least because everyone seems intent on persuading you to try them.

It's hard to say no to something when all your friends are doing it. This kind of stress comes in all types of forms. Your friends may say it's OK for you to say no, and then act as if it isn't, maybe they make you feel boring for not trying things out or perhaps, you just don't like being the odd one out. Drink and drugs aren't a solution to any of these problems. They won't make you more confident or mature, or make you feel you fit in more, in fact, they'll have the opposite effect. Remember, taking substances doesn't prove you're a better friend, only one that can't stand up for yourself.

DE-STRESS TIPS:

- Remember, real friends won't encourage you to do something dangerous, they will protect you and stand by you even when you disagree with them.

- Involvement with drink and drugs presents serious problems. Saying 'no' at the outset will eradicate a whole host of potential stresses.
- Saying 'no' and not following the crowd will earn you respect. It shows you have self-confidence and indepedence.

THE STRESS: "It's uncool to be a swot."

School for many people is a nightmare. If you're not worrying about work pressure and exams, there's your peers to deal with. School is often seen as uncool and therefore if you happen to be someone who works hard, the pressure is probably on to make you back off. However, it's worth realising that if you do this the only life you'll be ruining is yours.

While it's stressful to be someone who cares about his or her marks, it's more stressful not to be. Remember, you have a few more years of learning to be done. You can choose to do nothing and complain every day, or you can make the best of it.

The last method has the advantage that you're going to get a lot further in your life if you have a few qualifications behind you. You never know where you're going to end up in the future and you don't yet know what you will need and what you won't.

DE-STRESS TIPS:

- Work out what you want from life, and stick to it.
- If you're being bullied seek help from your family and teachers.
- If you work hard, you'll have the last laugh.

● CHAPTER THREE ●

School stress

"I hate school. My teachers pick on me and tell me I don't try hard enough. They say I should work harder but what's the point."

Gary (14)

"The girls in my class really get me down. They say bitchy things about me and make fun of my voice. Sometimes I get so miserable I pretend I am sick so I don't have to go to school and face them."

Heather (13)

"My parents are always saying, you've got to work hard and do well in your exams. I feel like I am under all this pressure from them and I am worried that I'm going to let them down."

Jill (13)

The largest source of stress for most young people is school. Not only are there exams, teachers and homework to contend with, but also a whole multitude of stresses from your friends and peers.

Hardly surprising then that many young people are so unhappy at school and can't wait to leave.

Every Sunday night you may get a feeling in the pit of your stomach – a churning, sick feeling – because you know the next day you have to go back to school and relive your week all over again.

One year, I was lucky enough to get a great teacher. Someone who understood the way many of us seemed to feel. He gave us the following tips about how to cope with the stresses of school life:

1   You don't have to be good at all your subjects, but it makes your life easier if you at least try.
2   It's not the end of the world if you fail an exam.
3   Don't listen to people who tell you you're no good at something and that you can't be whatever you want to be.
4   Teachers don't know everything.
5   Ask if you need help, teachers are there for your benefit.
6   Ignore the people you don't get on with. Once you're out of school you never have to see them again.
7   Everyone is good at something.
8   Qualifications are your ticket to do whatever you want in life, not just a piece of paper.

WHEN YOU DON'T WANT TO GO TO SCHOOL

Everyone has days or even weeks, when they don't want to go to school and consider bunking off.

Rather than giving in to your feelings you need to determine exactly what's making you hate school:

- Is the work too hard for you?
- Are you bored?
- Do you feel you have no friends?
- Are you being picked on?
- Do you hate your teachers?

Ask yourself which of the above are stressing you out. Then make a list of all the things you dislike about school and why. Your next step is to consider what you can do (besides skipping school) to solve the situation.

If the work's too hard, speak to your teacher. Ask for help and consider extra classes. If you're bored, it could be that the classes are too easy for you or that you are doing the wrong subjects for your personality. Rather than letting these things stress you out and make you unhappy, focus instead on doing something positive about it (refer to page 39 to find out how to zap school stress).

THE SCHOOL POPULARITY CONTEST

"There are these girls in my school and they are so cool. They're pretty, wear great clothes and the boys love them. I'd love to be friends with them, but they ignore me. They think I'm a geek and there's no way they'd let me hang out with them."

Jacqui (13)

Whether we like it or not, the friends we have influence our lives and the way we feel about ourselves. If you're lucky enough to have a good group of friends, you'll already know this. However, if you're on your own or wish you belonged to another group of friends it's likely your school days are pretty stressful and sometimes miserable. School is not a popularity contest, but it sometimes feels like one, especially if you're not one of the 'popular' people.

There's more to life than being popular at school, but if the popular people are making your life miserable, it's time to look at what's stressing you out and how you can deal with it:

1. They ignore you

It's never nice being ignored, especially when you feel that you've done nothing wrong. It can make even the most down-to-earth person feel lonely and invisible.

If you feel like this, it might help to realise the sad truth about cliques – they look far more exciting than they actually are. For starters, they are usually made up of one leader and a group of scared followers. Secondly, they get their power by giving others the impression that they are better than everyone else, when in fact they are no better. Look at it this way and you'll see that to be ignored by them means very little.

It doesn't mean that you're not cool enough, trendy enough or pretty enough to join their group. In fact, it usually means you're smart enough to stand up for yourself and wise enough to know there's no fun to be had in being bossed around.

2. They bully you

Believe it or not, there is no rhyme or reason as to why certain people get bullied, and bullying can take many different forms. The result is always the same – stress and misery. Childline receives over 20,000 calls a year from people with bullying and school problems, so you're not alone.

If you're being bullied, don't suffer in silence. Always seek help from your family, teachers and friends. Bullying destroys self-confidence and self-esteem. It has a lasting effect on the victim and years later many people still admit how defeated they feel by events that took place years ago.

3. They label you a geek

If you're not labelled one of the popular people at school, it's likely you've been given a different tag. Maybe one that's flattering and you're happy with it, or perhaps it's one that isn't and you hate it. Horrible as it is to be categorised, it's not worth stressing over because it's likely that the person who has labelled you doesn't know you at all. A label is just someone else's opinion and nothing else. Even if it is true, tell yourself – so what? Many of the most successful people in the world today were labelled geeks or swots at school, and look at them now!

ZAP THE STRESS

- Ignore the names other people call you.
- Be true to yourself.
- Be friends with people you truly like, not those you think you should be friends with.
- Do what's best for you, and not what a 'friend' tells you.

EXAM PRESSURE

"Just the thought of exams makes me feel sick and panicky. I hate them and I hate the fact that I have to take so many. What can I do to help myself?"

Karen (14)

"I'm not good at anything. Not only do I fail all my exams, but all my parents do is go on and on at me about how I am going to ruin my life and end up without a job."

Sarah (14)

No matter what other people say, exams are not the most important thing you will ever do in your life. And while they are a necessity, they are not worth getting depressed over.

So the next time you feel sick with stress and near to despair, remind yourself of the following:

- Pass or fail, you are more than a grade on a piece of paper.

- If you fail an exam, you can take it again.
- It's not the end of the world if you don't get a high grade.
- If you feel you can't cope with the stress of taking an exam, ask for help ASAP.
- If your parents are adding to your anxiety, tell them so. They may think they are helping you.
- Not all successful people were great at exams.
- Tell yourself it's only a test, nothing more.
- Study, but give yourself breaks. Not only will this help you to retain more information, but it will also help you to keep a healthy perspective.

PARENTS AND EXAMS

Parental expectations can be the root of a lot of school work stress and anxiety. If your parents are the kind of people who's idea of encouragement is to always be on your case, nagging you to study more and work harder, it may be time to tell them how they're making you feel:

- Explain your fears and anxieties to them. This is often the best way to get them to understand that they are not helping you.
- Tell them what you find encouraging and what you don't.
- If they still won't listen, try getting a teacher or relative to speak to them.

Remember, you can only do your best and even the most pushy parent knows that. Don't do your worst just to get back at your parents as this will only add to your stress levels.

ZAPPING SCHOOL STRESS

Don't let school get you down

Believe it or not, school is not there to make you unhappy and sick with stress. It's there to help you find your way in the world, through learning and social interaction. If you're not getting this message, it's likely you need some advice and support in your school life. If so, start by talking to your parents or a teacher you trust, and remember, nothing is ever so bad it can't be resolved.

Dealing with your teachers

Teachers can actually help you to change your life. OK, some of them don't bring out the best in you, but many really would like to help. If there's a teacher you like, try to see what qualities make you like them and try to apply this to the rest of your teachers.

If there is one teacher picking on you – don't just put up with it. Make a note of your complaints and do something about it. Teachers are there to help you, not to pick on you or make your life miserable.

Coping with subjects you hate

Feeling useless at a particular subject such as sport, maths or science can affect your whole life. If you feel this way about a subject, try to pin-point the exact reason why it gets you down. Once you've done this – work out how you can rectify things by asking yourself: Do you need more help? Do you need to ask more questions? Do you need to study more? Then look at the subjects you are good at. Remember, no one is expecting you to be brilliant at all subjects.

10 WAYS TO LOWER YOUR STRESS LEVELS AT SCHOOL

1 Work to the best of your abilities.
2 Remind yourself you are not in competition with every person in your class.
3 If you find something tough, ask for help.
4 Don't leave your work to the last minute.
5 Don't blow your exams out of proportion.
6 Don't let your parents load on the pressure.
7 Remind yourself school doesn't last forever.
8 Surround yourself with people who genuinely like you.
9 Refuse to accept labels other people give you.
10 Decide what you can get out of school, and go for it.

CHAPTER FOUR

Body stress

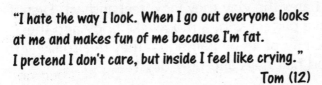

"I hate the way I look. When I go out everyone looks at me and makes fun of me because I'm fat.
I pretend I don't care, but inside I feel like crying."

Tom (12)

"One time, these guys started laughing at me on the bus, and calling me bean pole because I'm really tall and skinny. I was so upset I got off the bus and walked home. Now I feel so stressed out about my looks that I just don't want to go out any more. I'd rather sit at home, where no one makes fun of me."

Lisa (13)

"I am so ugly, I know no one will ever want to go out with me. And even though I'm a nice person it doesn't count for much when it comes to falling in love."

Heather (14)

If you are concerned about your appearance, ask yourself the following questions:

- How many times have you looked in the mirror and groaned at what's looked back at you?
- How many times have you felt close to tears because you hate the way you look?
- Do you worry more than once a day that you're too fat, too thin, too short or too tall?
- Are you critical of yourself and others?

If you've answered 'yes' to the any of the above, then you're normal! At one time or another, every single person hates the way they look, feel and act. Even if they have perfect skin, a model-like body and the facial beauty of an oil painting – they're also likely to have bad hair days and ugly days!

Even if they are well co-ordinated, stylish and sporty, they are just as likely to fall on their face as you and me. The real key to working out if you're really stressed-out about these things is to notice how often your 'bad' days occur. If they happen once a month, don't worry, but if they've become regular occurrences or every day feelings, then it's time to take control and zap the stress.

STRESS ONE: PUBERTY STRIKES

"I feel I don't have control of my body. All of a sudden, I've become much bigger and taller than my friends. My mum says I should feel glad, but I don't. I feel embarrassed and huge. It makes me want to hide where no one can see me."

Liz (14)

We've all heard the saying – love yourself and others will too, and though this is true, it often doesn't feel true, especially when your body is exploding out in different directions. This weird rapid growth process is known as puberty and it happens to us all.

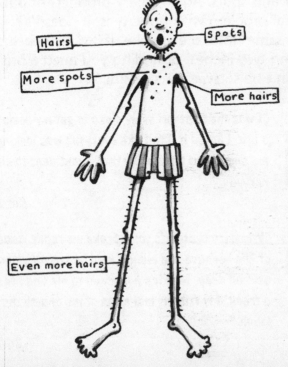

Look around you. There is bound to be someone who has suddenly shot up in height or put on weight. And someone who has spots over their face, or a girl who has grown breasts. This is not an alien mutation, but puberty working it's magic spell, and transforming you from a child into an adult.

While puberty is a natural and normal thing, it's also a time when many people feel stressed and conscious about their looks, height and weight.

Girls in particular feel anxious about their weight because their body starts naturally developing and laying down fat (essential for periods). Boys feel conscious about the growth of their body hair, their height and spots. Again, all by-products of puberty. The real problem with puberty is, it doesn't happen at the same time to everyone. If it did, then suddenly growing two inches, or finding you need a bra wouldn't be so scary or stressful.

 "I was the first girl in my class to get my period and a bra. I hated it. I felt like everyone was looking at me and I went from being really confident to shy and nervous."

Sarah (14)

 *"When my brother's voice broke we really made fun of him because one minute he'd be squeaky and the next all deep. Now it's happened to me and I feel like a freak. My friends make fun of me and all the girls laugh."*

Gavin (12)

If being one of the first to start puberty, or one of the last, is stressing you out, the important thing to realise is eventually everyone will go through this process and have to deal with what you're dealing with. And remember, without these changes you'd never become an adult.

If you look at your body changes this way you'll see that there's very little to get stressed out about. Tell yourself this every time you notice a spot or a stretch mark and it will stop you feeling bad or paranoid over something which is perfectly natural and normal.

STRESS TWO: WEIGHT STRESS

"I look at my body every morning and cry. I am so fat and horrible to look at, and the worse thing is I never used to be this way. Now I dread PE or any class where I have to stand up in front of everyone. I spend my days thinking of ways to get out of going to school."

Tanya (13)

Does this quote sound familiar? If it does, it may help you to realise that between the ages of 10 and 16 years old you are destined to gain weight. Why? Well, it's actually got very little to do with a burger overload and a lot to do with your hormones. During puberty, your hormones are responsible for laying fat all over your body. While most of us love to hate this fat, it's actually 100% essential for growth and healthy bones. It's role is to coat the body's cells, cushion the organs from damage, and stop the cold from getting in. Once deposited, this fat then supplies the body with the energy and fuel it needs to do everyday things like walking and dancing.

While this makes logical sense, it may not help you to feel stress-free about your body, especially if you don't feel you're at the 'right' weight.

It is unhealthy and can be potentially dangerous to be at a weight were you deny yourself food, feel ill and tired all the time or try to be the same weight as a friend.

The fact is, we are all unique, and this means we're all destined to have a different weight, size and shape. Some people will be born thin and leggy while others will be shorter and broader – it's all a matter of genes. Like it or not, genes are the growth map that play a vital role in determining what we'll look like.

However, if you're really unsure about your weight, and think you're overweight, consider these questions:

1 Does your body weight restrict you from doing what you want to do?
2 Do you get out of breath just walking up the stairs?
3 When you run for a bus does your heart feel as if it's going to burst?

And if you're unsure about your weight, and think you're underweight, consider these questions:

1 Are you tired all the time?
2 Do you fall ill a lot?
3 Do you sometimes feel faint?

Three 'yes's' and you're probably not at your healthy weight. You need to see your doctor and start eating healthily.

So, where does all the anxiety about weight come from? Eating should be one of the great pleasures in life and yet, because of the messages we all receive about fat and food, many people find it a battle-ground.

We learn negative beliefs from the messages we pick up from our friends, families and the media. However, it's important to move your focus away from what others tell you about your body and weight and instead learn to look at what is most healthy for you – both physically and emotionally.

Zap the stress of eating by:

- Not forbidding yourself certain foods.
- Eating a balanced, healthy diet.
- Being aware that high sugar foods like sweets and cakes can actually make you feel depressed after eating them. This is because the sugar content of these foods affects your body's mood regulator.
- Asking yourself – am I really hungry? Rate your need to eat on a scale of 1 to 5. If you score between 1–3 then you probably don't need to eat.
- Dividing foods into good and bad things. Balance is the key to healthy eating.
- Refusing to compare what you eat to what your friends eat.

STRESS THREE: HATING THE WAY YOU LOOK

"I can't bear the way I look so I never look in a mirror. The one in my bedroom is balanced against the wall so I can't see my face in it."

Karis (14)

"Everyone is so trendy and I'm not. I don't have the same clothes as my friends and I never look good like them."

Jo (13)

For some people, the mirror equals a living nightmare because what they see looking back at them makes them feel depressed, upset, and even sometimes suicidal. If you're someone who shys away from having their picture taken, winces when they see their reflection and feels that somehow they are not matching up to others, then horrible as it sounds, it's time to make friends with yourself!

Part of the stress of avoiding looking at yourself is imagining you're worse than you actually are. This is why the first step in coming to terms with what's actually in front of you, is to make yourself look at your reflection.

1 Start by looking in the mirror for 2 minutes. At first you'll be flooded with negative messages you've been telling yourself for months. However, after a while your mind will get bored of putting you down and will start looking for good things. Help yourself by focusing on what you like and when you've found three pleasing things, write them down. Aim to add one more thing to this list each day.

2   Ask your friends and family to say what they like best about you. Do not question their answers or shrug off their compliments and imagine they are only 'being nice'. Instead, practice accepting what they say and add them to your list. Now, look in the mirror again and try to see what they see in you.

3   Every time you look in the mirror, make it a rule that the first thing you'll say is something nice to yourself.

4   Pin your list to your mirror to remind yourself that you are much more than your negative thoughts. Positive thoughts work the same way as negative thoughts: the more you say them, the more you'll believe them.

Remember looks aren't everything. Everyone has bad days, and if you're in the midst of one, remind yourself tomorrow is a new day.

STRESS FOUR: SELF-ESTEEM

"I wish I was pretty because then I know my life would be happier and I wouldn't feel such a freak. I look at famous people and they are all pretty. It proves you need to be good-looking to get by in life."

Suzanne (13)

A clever wit once said, 'compare yourself to others and you risk feeling unattractive or smug' – neither of which are great feelings. Are you someone guilty of this? If so, it's time to take the pressure off.

Firstly, not all famous people are beautiful, it's the attractive qualities of their lives which makes them appear beautiful. Think of 10 famous people and imagine them at your age, doing the things you do. Are they so beautiful now? If they were normal people would you put so much emphasis on their looks? I doubt it.

Self-esteem is basically the way you feel about yourself. If you feel any of the following, your self-esteem probably needs boosting:

1 You never feel you're good enough.
2 You imagine everyone is more interesting and more attractive than you.
3 You have feelings of self-disgust about your body.
4 Sometimes when you look at your reflection you feel like crying.
5 You imagine everyone is laughing at you.
6 You feel no one understands what you're going through.
7 You don't remember the good things people say about you, only the bad.
8 You wish you were someone else.

Boost your self-esteem by:

• Writing a list of all the good things you possess, both physical and non-physical and stick it to your mirror. Read it twice a day.
• Speaking out if you don't like a particular label a friend has given you. Laughing along and trying to ignore it doesn't work, it just makes people think they can tease you even more.

- Confronting someone who puts you down.
- Be realistic about famous people. Don't imagine they have perfect lives – they don't.
- Focus on your own life. Think of ways you can improve the way you feel about yourself. Be proactive – if you hate it that you're unfit, take up some exercise. If you want to know more about something, visit the library. Don't let others hold you back, and more importantly, don't hold yourself back. You can do anything you set your mind to.

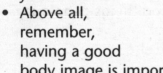

- Above all, remember, having a good body image is important because it's a vital part of your self-confidence. If you hate the way you look and feel, then you won't project yourself in a positive way to people you meet. Stand up straight, smile and tell yourself, 'I'm a great person and I'm worth knowing'.

● QUIZ ●

BEAUTY OR BEAST – HOW DO YOU REALLY SEE YOURSELF?

When it comes to feeling good about yourself are you someone who can let the compliments flow or your own worst enemy? Here's five questions to find out for sure:

1 **You pass a shop window displaying a fabulously slinky outfit. What do you do?**
   a) Wonder if you could get into it with a bit of exercise.
   b) Think of all your friends and how good they'd look in it, then get depressed about your own body.
   c) Go and try it on.

2 **You walk past a mirror. Do you?**
   a) Check your reflection out of the corner of your eye and then wish you hadn't.
   b) Look the other way so you don't catch sight of your body.
   c) Look to see if you're looking great.

3 **How many parts of your body do you hate?**
   a) More than five
   b) One or two
   c) Less than five

4 Which one of the following fills you most with dread?

a) Having to get up on stage and speak in front of the whole school.

b) Having to wear a swimming costume in front of people you know.

c) Having to go shopping on a Saturday with your mum.

5 If you had one wish what would it be?

a) That you looked like a model.

b) That you had gorgeous hair.

c) That you looked more normal.

SCORES

1.	a 5	b 0	c 10
2.	a 5	b 0	c 10
3.	a 0	b 10	c 5
4.	a 5	b 0	c 10
5.	a 0	b 10	c 5

0 – 20

You have quite low self esteem and are letting it get you down so much so that it's causing stress overload in your life. You need to boost your confidence levels by looking at your good points (and we all have them) and not getting hung up on the way other people, especially famous people look.

25 – 35

You're doing pretty well. You're prone to self esteem off days which in turn stress you out. When these kick in, instead of giving in to them you need to recognise them for what they are and focus on the positive things you like about yourself.

40 – 50

You're pretty savvy on the self esteem front – you don't let negative thoughts get you down. Good on you, keep up the good work.

CHAPTER FIVE

Family stress

"When I get in from school my parents start on me. Nagging me about my room, shouting because I haven't helped around the house and generally telling me I am useless. It gets me down to the point where I just want to run away."

Paul (13)

"My mum and dad argue all the time, it really upsets me. They got divorced three years ago and even though I was sad at the time, I was also relieved because it meant no more fights. But now every time dad comes to pick us up on Fridays, they carry on again. It always ends with mum crying and dad making us get in the car. It's got to the point where I just dread weekends."

Heather (14)

"There are times when I just get so mad. My dad is always telling me to be careful and not to do this and that. It's like he doesn't trust me or something."

Dan (13)

Out of all the many stress sources in the world, your family probably rate amongst the highest (Childline actually receives nearly 15,000 calls a year from people with family problems). Love them or loathe them, all families cause each other mountains of stress and agitation.

Think about it, these are the people who can (and probably do) push all your wrong buttons, tease you till you cry, or cause you stress by the way they behave around you.

Perhaps your family fight all the time and use you as a weapon in their battles. Maybe they treat you badly, or ignore you. Whatever the source of your family stress, it's important to realise you're not alone.

HOW YOUR PARENTS CAN STRESS YOU OUT

1. Criticism

The most obvious ways your parents can stress you out is through criticism. They may make you feel lazy, stupid, ugly or a nuisance. Being made to feel not good enough will only lead to more stress, anxiety and tension at home, and will ruin your long-term confidence.

If you find you're nervous around a parent or worried all the time that you're letting them down, it can help to understand where their criticism is coming from:

WHY THEY CRITICISE

- They could be hard on you because they are hard on themselves.
- They may see their criticisms as encouragement.
- They might think you're not living up to what you could be.
- They might be unable to deal with the fact you've become a person with your own views and thoughts.
- They may think you don't take their words to heart.
- They might not even realise they are doing it.

WHAT TO DO

To combat any or all of the above, you need to say something now before it goes too far.

The next time they criticise you:

- Tell them how their words make you feel about yourself.

- Explain you need positive, not negative encouragement.
- Show them you are doing your best.
- Ask them why they feel the need to always yell at you.

If you are being compared to an older brother or sister, don't fall into the trap of trying to be like him/her. It won't work. You are a unique individual with your own strengths and talents.

2. Have too high expectations

"My parents want me to be a teacher. I want to tell them I'm not clever enough and I can't do half my work, but I'm scared they'll be really disappointed in me. So, I pretend that I'm doing better than I actually am."

Caroline (15)

"My exam results have just come back and I'm terrified to show them to my parents because I've done so badly. I'm scared and worried because they're going to be mad at me."

Anon (15)

There's nothing quite so stressful as living with parents who have high expectations of you. When this happens you can end up feeling alienated, alone and pretty desperate when things go wrong.

WHY THEY HAVE HIGH EXPECTATIONS

- Parents who push usually do so because they want you to reach your full potential.

- They may feel no one pushed them and so they have to push you.
- They may want you to be like them.
- They may feel you're not trying hard enough.
- They may be passing on their own frustrations or regrets of their own life.

WHAT TO DO

- Explain how their expectations make you feel when you're studying – panic-ridden, anxious, helpless, scared, etc.
- Do not let your parents plan your future without your consent.
- Don't take on their expectations, just do your best.
- Don't imagine it's the end of the world if you fail something – it isn't.
- Talk to someone outside the family about the stress your parents are putting you under.

COMMON TYPES OF FAMILY STRESS

1. Wanting the perfect family

"I hate my family. My dad's lazy, my mum moans all the time and my sisters are an embarrassment. Everyone thinks I am just like them, but I'm not. Why can't they be different."

Susie (13)

Hands up if you've got the perfect family? A family which never argues, is always kind to each other and understands when things go wrong. In reality, most families get on each other's nerves, make mistakes and say the wrong thing. You can't choose your family, so make the most of what you've got.

2. Parents who argue all the time

"I think my mum and dad hate each other. They act like they do anyway. They call each other names, throw things and say they wish each other were dead. It's horrible having to live like this. I just lock myself in my room and play my music really loud so I don't have to listen to it."

Lisa (13)

Most people in relationships argue. It can be upsetting to watch your parents argue every day, but if it's getting you down you have to talk to them. Get your worries out in the open and it might make them think twice about their behaviour. If that doesn't work think about asking someone to mediate – a family friend, a relative or another adult who can help your parents to see how they are affecting you.

3. Parents who separate

"My dad left home six months ago. I keep waiting for him to come back, but he hasn't. Sometimes he visits and I try to make him stay, but he just says he can't and then cries. My mum cries too and then I feel I've done something terrible. I don't understand what's going on."

Sarah (14)

Try to see that if your parents separate or divorce it has nothing to do with anything you have said or done. Parents don't leave each other because of their children, but because they don't love each other any more. So, if your parents are separated or divorced, remember, they will always be your mother and father whether they are 'officially' together or not. And if you feel scared and stressed by what's happening or what has happened, talk to your parents and tell them how much everything worries you. Let them reassure you that just because they've fallen out of love with each other, it doesn't mean they'll ever fall out of love with you.

4. Parents who aren't around

"My dad doesn't want to know me any more. Since he left my mum he has re-married and never calls or sends me a birthday card. I try not to let my mum know I'm upset, but inside I feel really bad. I keep wondering what I've done to make him act like this."

Karis (14)

There is often an emotional reason behind parents who act like this, for instance, guilt or not being able to face your unhappiness. Other times, financial or practical reasons can keep you apart from your parents.

Don't waste your time thinking, 'If I were a better person they would have stuck around.' The sad truth is, some parents can't cope with having responsibilities and would rather walk away than stay and make it work.

6. Over-protective parents

"My parents drive me crazy, they quiz me on everything from where I am going to who I'll be with. They insist on me being home by 9pm, and they won't let me do anything. This means I have to lie to them otherwise I'd lose all my friends."

Liz (14)

If you feel that your parents are over-protective, you have to show them that they can trust you. Lying about where you're going, coming home late and hanging out with troublemakers won't exactly instill confidence in your parents.

If you're mad at them because they won't let you live your life, then talk to them about it. Try and reach a compromise, for instance, promise to be in by 9pm one week and ask them to gradually increase the time in the following weeks.

A WORD ABOUT ABUSE

Family abuse comes in lots of different forms.
It occurs when adults hurt young people, either
physically or emotionally. There are four main areas of
abuse. Physical – which includes hitting, kicking,
punching and burning. Emotional – which includes
threats, swearing and generally undermining your
confidence. Neglect – when basic needs such as food,
warmth, shelter and medical care are not given.
Sexual – when an adult pressurises or forces a young
person to take part in any kind of sexual activity.
All forms of abuse are damaging and no matter the
reason for it, you need to seek help from a trusted
adult, teacher or outside organisation immediately
(refer to Useful Contacts).

YOUR PARENTS' STRESS LEVELS

It's worth pointing out here that you're not the only
one who gets stressed out by family life. Your
parents will also be under a huge amount of stress
usually made worse by their jobs and daily pressures.
In some people this stress can build up to frightening
levels. If you feel that one or both of your parents can
no longer cope, you need to seek help (refer to Useful
contacts).

ZAP FAMILY STRESS

- Communicate with your family, don't just yell.
- Respect the fact that your parents are likely to be
  under a great deal of pressure themselves.

- Don't blame your family for everything.
- Stand up for yourself and for what you believe is right (this doesn't mean refusing to listen).
- Don't take out your bad moods on your family.
- Take time out. If you feel angry or on the point of exploding, go somewhere quiet where you can count to 10.
- Make your life easier by not being secretive and lying about what you do.
- Try not to take everything your parents say as a potential insult and don't be defensive every time they say something.
- If they say something that is hurtful, tell them.
- Keep your sibling jealousy in check – by reminding yourself you are not in competition.

SIBLING STRESS

"My parents always say, 'Why can't you be like your brother Paul, he's so great at this and so good at that'. They mean that I'm a failure and they wish I was different."

Callum (13)

"My sister really gets on my nerves. She is always taking my things, borrowing my clothes and hanging on to me and my friends. My mum says it's because she wants to be like me, but I hate it. I feel like I am babysitting her all the time."

Amy (12)

"My brother teases me all the time. He calls me fatty and pig face and thinks it's really funny. It's not and when I tell my parents they say I should just ignore it or tell me off for being a telltale."

Susie (14)

Jealousy is a very powerful emotion. It eats away at our self-confidence, makes us feel weak, useless and thoroughly miserable. Unfortunately, the first time most of us experience this emotion is with one of our siblings. Hardly surprising when you think about it, after all – these are the first people we learn to have proper relationships with.

The answer to sibling rivalry is simply to admit that you are different, but to realise that this doesn't mean one of you is better than the other. If your parents make you feel as if you are in competition, tell them how you feel and how discouraged it makes you. If one sibling is making your life miserable, tell your parents and see if you can sort the problem out.

There is a fine line between teasing and bullying. Teasing is supposed to be playful, but of course, if it's done constantly it can eventually feel quite hurtful.

They may be teasing you to annoy you, or for fun because they don't realise it's impact. If this is the case, tell them it hurts your feelings, it's ruining your confidence and making you feel stressed. Look for a compromise – they tease less, and you won't take it too seriously.

If you happen to have a younger brother or sister who copies you – don't be too hard on them. Annoying as it is, having someone copy you is also a big compliment. If you want it to stop, why not offer to help them find their own look. Once they have this, then they'll have the confidence to be themself and not just a pale imitation of you.

CHAPTER SIX

Stress management

By this stage you should be pretty knowledgeable about who and what causes stress, and what to do about it. However, apart from learning to notice what's going on and talking about your feelings, there is one more way you can manage stress in your life. That's by taking responsibility for your own part in it.

The fact is, sometimes when life gets too much it's easy to react in a way which intensifies the problem, rather than defuses it. This is known as an 'inappropriate response' – a reaction that is exaggerated and exceeds the actual event.

For example, your dad asks you to do something, and immediately you react with fury. Maybe because he's interrupting you or because you feel he's always asking you to do things. He then feels angry with you for refusing to listen to his need for help, and the situation deteriorates into an argument. This causes stress levels to rise all round and turns a seemingly simple encounter into a needlessly painful affair, with both of you ending up annoyed, upset and stressed.

So you can see that an inappropriate response can cause trouble. This is why it's important to look at your reactions and see how you can manage them more effectively.

● QUIZ ●

HOW DO YOU REACT TO STRESS?

1 It's your birthday and you're supposed to be going to the cinema but your best friend lets you down at the last minute because they have a date. What do you do?
   a) Confront your friend.
   b) Refuse to speak to them.

Answer A is the appropriate response because your friend has let you down and you have the right to express how you feel. By choosing option B, you are extending the situation and leaving yourself open to weeks of stress and upset, before you finally confront them.

2 You're on the computer when your mum comes in and asks you to come downstairs and help her with dinner. You ...
   a) Ignore her – after all, she can see you're busy.
   b) Grumble and follow her.

Answer B is the most appropriate response because you probably don't want to give up what you're doing, but know you have to. Ignoring her will exacerbate the situation and cause more trouble.

3 An important set of exams are coming up. You have worked for them but you feel ...
   a) Worried that you might fail.
   b) Sick because you don't know what you're going to do when you fail, and what your parents will say.

Answer A is the appropriate response because exams are worrying and most people do feel anxious about taking them. B is inappropriate because it's guessing at the future and adding unnecessary stress to an already stressful situation.

4 All your friends have a boyfriend or girlfriend. You think ...
   a) Am I ever going to meet someone?
   b) I can't bear being on my own forever.

Answer A is a better answer because it adopts a positive outlook, whereas B assumes the worse, making you feel as if this has already happened.

COMMON RESPONSES TO STRESS

1. Chronic worrying

"I find myself worrying all the time about everything. If it's not about what I've done and said, it's about the future and what's going to happen. I worry that my parents will be disappointed in me, and that my friends will stop liking me and I worry that I'll never get a boyfriend. Sometimes I actually feel sick about the thought of all this."
Sarah (14)

Chronic worriers are people who worry constantly about everything. They do this because they think by anticipating everything that could go wrong they will avoid risk. The problem is no one can anticipate everything, and worrying is usually worse than the real thing.

Worrying adds stress to your life because it makes you imagine all kinds of horrible scenarios that aren't real. Think of it as living in 'what if – land':

- What if ... I fail my exams.
- What if ... she dumps me.
- What if ... my parents split up.
- What if ... I never get a boyfriend or girlfriend.
- What if ... I can't get a job.

When this happens, you make yourself live through things that haven't even happened and focus on the feelings and reactions you may have. The end result of which is panic, anxiety and possible sickness.

ZAPPING THE STRESS OF WORRYING

- Forget the past, and don't ponder on the future.
- Choose to live in the present moment and enjoy it.
- Every time you feel yourself worrying, bring yourself right into the moment by concentrating on your breathing. Then immediately think of five things you feel happy about.
- Instead of letting your mind race, focus on what people are saying to you – let yourself be reassured.
- Talk about your worries, doing this can make you realise how futile or unlikely your worries are.

2. Anger

"Sometimes I just feel so angry and annoyed. I feel myself getting all worked up and irritated. Then I can't release it and sit there fuming and feeling like I am going to explode."

Toni (13)

What makes you angry? Someone barging past you on the bus; a friend gossiping about you; a TV programme, or a boyfriend or girlfriend who won't say 'I love you'?

If any of the above stir something in you then you'll probably recognise the following physical reactions to anger: your body starts to feel hot and flushed; you sweat, your throat, chest and jaw will become tense;

your heart will pound and your breathing becomes faster. This is all because your body is gearing up to take action. Unfortunately, most people do not take action, they try to swallow their anger and repress it which means the anxiety and stress stay bubbling below the surface. The fact is, being angry with someone you love, like your parents, a sibling or a best friend is a normal healthy emotion when you feel that you've been treated unfairly.

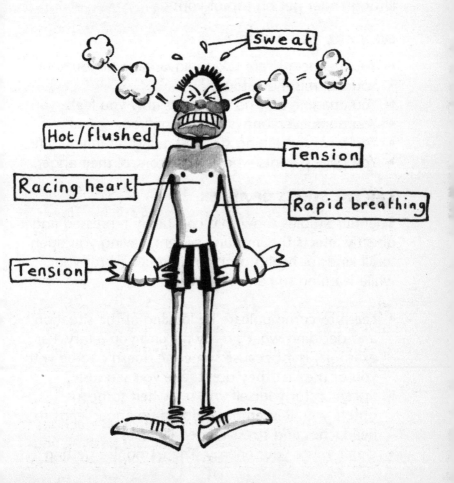

Sweat

Hot/flushed

Tension

Racing heart

Rapid breathing

Tension

Sometimes, this unfairness will have been on purpose and your anger will be justified. Other times, your anger will be the result of a misunderstanding or a difference of opinion. While anger is a normal emotion, it's also a scary one because of where it can lead.

If you find yourself getting angry frequently, or you fly into a rage over the simplest things, it's likely you're letting anger get on top of you.

WHY ARE YOU ANGRY?

- You feel people are taking advantage of you.
- You feel misunderstood.
- You imagine that no one cares how you feel.
- You think everyone is picking on you.
- You have something stressful going on in your life.
- You have parents who cannot control their anger.

ZAP THE STRESS OF ANGER

Scientific studies show that constantly repressed anger directly affects the immune system leaving you open to all kinds of health problems. So, it's worth your while learning to control how you feel:

- Learn to communicate by looking at the situation and deciding what's really making you angry. For example, is it because someone doesn't agree with you or the fact they don't take you seriously?
- Speak up for yourself and say when someone upsets you. Remember, bottled-up anger leads to headaches and stress-related illnesses.
- Don't waste your energy. There's no use getting

mad just because the bus is late or you've lost something. If you lose your cool over simple things no one will take you seriously when something is really wrong.

- Make sure your anger is justified.
- When you feel angry, count to ten slowly before you say something. This works because it allows you to think before you speak. Anger is often intensified by snap comments and judgements. Consider what is being said and done to you before reacting, and you're more likely to defuse the situation.
- Don't stew over things. If you're someone who stores up all the wrongs being done against you, you're more likely to act aggressively when someone adds to this. Instead of going over and over what's wrong – say something to the person who upset you.
- Channel your aggression into something positive, like a competitive sport, music, a journal or even your pillow.
- Talk about how you feel. Living with a high amount of anger is unhealthy and unnecessary.

3. Arguing

"My mum and I argue about everything. She hates my clothes, hair and friends. She says I'm cheeky, I don't work hard enough and that she doesn't like me very much. I don't care because I hate her most of the time."

Liz (14)

Having disagreements and arguments are normal especially with the people you know and love. However, if you find every conversation with your parents ends in an argument it's likely that a huge misunderstanding is the root cause.

Firstly, it may help to realise that it's not all your fault. Most parents have a tough time dealing with the fact that their children who used to listen to everything they said, now have a mind of their own. Which is why when you say something contrary to them you might be accused of, 'being cheeky' or 'making out you know everything'. Sound familiar? If it does, you also have to take some of the blame here. Tone of voice usually betrays what you say to someone, so if you're going to disagree with your parents, try to say it in a way that won't provoke more arguments. Likewise, tell them why you're angry. They are not mind readers and can't tell why sometimes a simple request gets such an over the top response from you.

WHY YOU ALWAYS FEEL LIKE ARGUING?

- You feel no one cares.
- You feel misunderstood.
- You feel no one listens to you.
- There's too much pressure in your life.

ZAPPING ANGER STRESS

- Write down a list of what is making you angry and stressed.
- Think about ways you can take the pressure off.
- Look at how you speak to people, not just how they speak to you.

- If you keep losing emotional control, ask for help.
- Don't always act on the defensive, not everyone is out to get you.
- Consider if anger is the most appropriate response to the situation before you lose it.

4. Guilt

"Why do I feel guilty all the time? I feel like I am always letting people in my life down, and not doing the right thing."

Suzanne (13)

Guilt is about feeling you can't be what someone wants you to be, and the truth is, many people specialise in both feeling guilty and making others feel guilty.

They snap at a person because they are stressed and have no time for whatever that person wants and then feel horrible about it. So horrible that they either beat themselves up about it or give in and do what they don't really want to do.

Other people feel to blame for the slightest thing that goes wrong, whether it's their fault or not. They feel guilty when they let people down and guilty when someone does something to upset them. Then there are the people who are particularly adept at making others feel guilty so they can get their own way. Maybe they act hurt, or cry or even imply that if you were a better person you'd do what they want.

In many cases, guilt is a learned behaviour, and it's likely one of your parents feels guilty all the time. The real trouble with guilt is it adds stress to your life, making you feel as if you're not a good person. But, like any overwhelming response you can break out of it and stop making yourself feel bad.

ZAP THE GUILT STRESS

- Stop taking responsibility for everyone else's unhappiness.
- Don't ponder on things that are in the past. We all act badly sometimes.
- Don't over analyse everything you do, say and think.
- Don't let people make you feel bad for doing what you want.
- Don't let other people's opinions of you rule your life.

5. Thinking negatively

Are you a glass half full or a glass half empty kind of person? If you've gone for the first option – glass half full – it's likely your a positive person. Someone who looks on the bright side and doesn't waste time pondering on all the things that could go wrong. However, maybe people accuse you of being too good to be true. If so, don't let their words get you down. The fact is, studies show that being positive about life lowers stress levels, and keeps you happier even if things do not always work out.

If you've gone for the glass half empty option – it's likely you're someone who tends to be negative about life. You expect the worst and then aren't surprised when it happens. Maybe you call yourself a realist – someone who's not afraid to consider the bad things. That's fair enough if you're happy with it, but the chances are life gets you down a bit more than someone who is positive.

Focus on negative 'what ifs' and you will feel that emotion. Focus on the positivity and you approach the same situation in a completely different way. Of course, it's not so easy to change from negativity to positivity, especially when your inner critic raises its ugly head!

"I know I put myself down, I can't help it. But every time I go to do something, I hear this voice telling me I can't do it and that I'm going to make a fool out of myself."

Amy (12)

The inner critic is the horrible voice that sabotages your confidence every time you want to try something new, or do something you're scared of. It's the voice that puts you down and stresses you out.

The most important thing to remember is no one is automatically good at something. It takes practice and perseverance to get things right. So, while it's natural to feel stressed and anxious about new ventures, don't make things worse by imagining you're going to fail or disappoint someone. These are stresses you are adding to the mixture, not normal stresses.

To silence your inner critic and zap the stress, try the following:

1 Accept this voice is coming from you. It may be a message or a belief you've picked up from a friend, parent or teacher, but you are the one who has taken it on and repeated it to yourself.
2 Replace your critic with an inner coach. A voice that spurs you on every time you feel scared or vulnerable.

3 Accept the voice is only your insecurity making it's opinion felt.
4 Be patient with yourself. We all make mistakes, we all say stupid things, fall over in public and make bad choices. It's not the end of the world – so don't believe it is.

5 Change your focus. Instead of thinking you can't do something, imagine how great it would be if you could. If you never try, you'll never know.

CHAPTER SEVEN

Depressed or stressed?

"Most days everything gets me down. My parents, school, even my friends stress me out and make me feel like I can't cope. I don't understand why. I just feel so sad, and everything people say makes it worse. Some days I even feel like my life's just not worth living any more."

Callum (13)

As you've probably guessed by now, it's normal to feel stressed when things go wrong. However, stress in itself is rarely the cause of long term unhappiness. This is because stress tends to be something that happens in small bursts, so one minute you feel out of control and pressurised, the next you feel calm again. For example, think of the exam period – you feel hassled, stressed, and pressurised. Then you take your exams, the pressure's off, and the stress and all it's accompanying anxiety disappears.

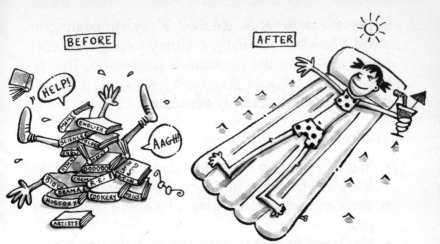

When anxiety levels never go down and you feel unhappy all the time, the chances are you could be depressed, rather than stressed (though stress obviously intensifies feelings of depression by adding to the general misery).

If you are suffering like this on a long-term basis, or know someone who is, it's worth knowing that you're not alone. There are literally thousands of young people across the country who feel desperate with misery every day. In fact, MIND (see page 103 for contact details), the leading mental health organisation estimates that one in eight teenagers suffer from depression in the UK. Statistics also show that at any one time, symptoms of depression will affect between 15 and 20% of the whole population.

UNHAPPY OR DEPRESSED?

However, before you swap one label for another and think you are

depressed rather than stressed, it's worth bearing in mind a few things. Firstly, contrary to popular belief, happiness is not the opposite of depression. That is to say that just because you don't feel happy, it doesn't mean you are necessarily depressed.

You're unhappy if ...

- You feel sad and miserable about a specific problem like a boyfriend or girlfriend leaving you.
- You can forget your sadness by doing something nice.
- You have an idea of what might make you feel better.
- You sometimes forget you're unhappy.

You're depressed if ...

- You feel numb to everything in your life.
- You feel a sense of hopelessness about everything.
- You can't really put your finger on what's wrong and why.
- You feel powerless.

COULD YOU BE DEPRESSED?

Try this small test and find out.

Answer 'yes' or 'no' to the following questions:

- You want to sleep all the time.
- You don't want to socialise any more.
- You feel life is pointless.
- You feel great anxiety.

- You've forgotten the last time you laughed.
- You feel you have nothing to offer.
- You feel totally alone.
- You've felt like this for longer than 2 weeks.

If you answer 'yes' to more than three, it's likely you are depressed and should talk to someone ASAP.

WHY DO PEOPLE GET DEPRESSED?

"Most days when I wake up, I feel like going back to bed because I can't cope. My mum says I have to snap out of it, but I can't. I can't concentrate, I can't sleep and all I want is to be left alone. Why do I feel like this?"

Karis (14)

People can become depressed for all kinds of reasons, some obvious, some not so obvious. Often, it's a combination of different things that cause it and these include:

- Psychological factors such as bullying, heartbreak and having a parent who is depressed.
- Social factors including peer pressure, exams, or money.
- Physical worries such as feeling too fat, or too thin.
- Traumatic events including a death in the family, divorce or becoming part of a new family.

Depression also varies from person to person. Some people feel so overwhelmed that normal everyday things like walking, talking and socialising become impossible. Others find they can behave perfectly well in front of friends and family, but inside they secretly feel terrified and alone.

Other symptoms of depression include:

- Disliking yourself mentally and physically.
- Hating others.
- Feeling out of tune with everyone else.
- Being negative about everything.
- Feeling empty and out of control.
- Feeling guilty.
- Losing interest in things that normally interested you.
- Not being able to make decisions.
- Wanting to be alone.
- Fatigue and irregular sleeping and eating patterns.
- Refusing to go to school.
- Feeling very moody.
- Acting recklessly.

People who suffer from depression also usually experience prolonged unhappiness, isolation, helplessness and despair. The real worry with depression is, it feeds on itself. So, if you leave it untreated it will only get far worse.

If you feel depressed and you just can't cope with daily life, you need to seek help. There is no miracle overnight cure for depression. However, learning how to release your pent-up feelings, changing aspects of your life that make you unhappy and finding ways to look forward to the future are all ways of combating your misery.

HOW TO HELP YOURSELF

If you feel as if you can't cope, you can help yourself by letting others help you.

Family and friends

Learning to talk to friends, family and loved ones is an important way of learning how to deal with your depression. These people can give you much needed support and help you to feel less isolated. However, if any of these people are the cause of your depression, or you feel you can't talk to them, try speaking to a trained and objective outsider such as a counsellor or psychotherapist.

Counsellor or psychotherapist

These people are trained to help you overcome your depression and help you find new ways of coping. Despite the stereotypical image of a 'shrink', seeing a counsellor doesn't mean that you are 'mad', or 'crazy'. It shows that you are tackling your problems head-on and not hiding from them. The best thing about counsellors and therapists is that they are completely confidential. This means you can say whatever you like to them and they cannot tell your parents without your consent.

Psychiatrists

Child psychiatrists deal with a wide range of mental health problems such as trauma, eating disorders, suicidal behaviour, phobias, anxieties and disruptive behaviour. Unlike therapists (who can also deal with these issues), they are also trained doctors and work usually in hospitals or guidance clinics under the NHS (you would have to be referred by your doctor).

Helplines

For those who feel very desperate or lonely there are a number of helplines available to give you free telephone counselling. These helplines are confidential and do not appear on your phone bill (refer to Useful contacts).

WHEN IT ALL GETS TOO MUCH – SEVERE DEPRESSION

"I want to kill myself. I hate my life, nothing ever goes right and there's no point to it any more. It's not a quick decision, I've been thinking of this for a long time."

Anon (15)

Always take your depression very seriously, because if it's left unchecked it may get worse and become potentially life threatening. As scary or as unreal as this thought is, it's worth noting that there are 19,000 suicide attempts by teenagers a year. That's one every 30 minutes! What's more, young men are particularly vulnerable because they are less likely to talk to someone about their feelings and fears.

If you feel like this, it's worth knowing that suicide is never the only option. There is no problem that can't be worked out. And no depression deep enough that can't be helped. Above all, there is always someone you can ask for help.

If you feel at all suicidal seek help. The Samaritans are on hand 24 hours a day, 365 days a year (refer to Useful contacts). Your doctor can also refer you on to someone who can help.

HELPING VERY DEPRESSED FRIENDS

"I have a friend who is always saying she's going to kill herself. She really annoys us because we know she just wants attention from us. How can we tell her to stop saying these things?"

Susie (14)

If you have a friend who talks about killing themselves, always take what they say seriously. It's a myth that people who talk about it don't attempt it. Other signs to watch out for are: severe depression, sudden manic behaviour, withdrawal from friends and family, and giving away prized possessions. If you want to show your friend that you care and you want to help, encourage them to seek help and to tell an adult (parent, teacher or counsellor) what is going on.

SOMETHING ELSE ALL TOGETHER

In certain cases, you'll find feeling depressed and stressed is about something else all together – usually a disorder that again is exacerbated by stress. Below are a few of the most common disorders that can make you feel stressed and low.

PHOBIAS

"I'm terrified of insects. I only have to see one and I think I'm going to be sick or faint."

Caroline (15)

A phobia is an irrational, but real fear of an object, animal or situation. When we say irrational, we mean the fear is out of proportion to the actual danger involved. For example, if you're afraid of spiders you may become so scared you imagine you're going to die, when the reality is the spider can do nothing to you.

The real problem with phobias is that phobics experience severe panic attacks when confronted with their fear. It doesn't even have to be the 'real' object that brings on a panic attack, sometimes the thought of it, a plastic replica, or picture can invoke the terror.

A recent study estimated that there are between five and seven million phobics in Britain. It is thought that most phobias are triggered in childhood or sometimes a phobia is 'learned' from a family member. Other phobias come in later life, for instance, Agoraphobia (fear of leaving your house) can happen when people have been ill for a long time or house bound for whatever reason.

There are many ways to treat a phobia; a popular method is De-sensitisation. The basic idea behind this method is to learn to face your fear head on, instead of running away from it. A trained Behavioural Therapist will help you do this. In the case of someone afraid of spiders, the phobic will be taught to relearn their ideas about spiders. The therapist may start with a picture of a spider, work towards a photograph, then introduce a plastic spider and then gradually work towards the phobic coping with a real one. Relaxation techniques are also given along the way to cope with anxiety (see page 8 for more information on panic attacks). For more information contact the PHOBICS SOCIETY (refer to Useful contacts).

OBSESSIVE COMPULSIVE DISORDERS (OCD)

"My sister is anorexic and has also been told she has OCD. Does this have something to do with why she's always washing her hands and the food she eats?"

Karen (14)

Obsessive Compulsive Disorder usually follows a period of intense stress. It is another phobia-like condition in which there are frequent repetitive rituals like washing your hands, checking that doors are locked and even dressing in a particular order every day. Sufferers feel they have to perform some action such as washing their hands to relieve their mounting tension and stress. They believe if they do these things they will be OK and the tension will go away.

OCD usually begins in adolescence or early adulthood. It affects up to 3% of the population and is characterised by obsessive thoughts, impulses and rituals.

Help can be found through your doctor who can refer you to a behavioural therapist who will use one of the above techniques (see Phobias).

SAD (SEASONAL AFFECTIVE DISORDER)

"My mum has something called SAD. What is it and why does she get so stressed out all the time?"

Gavin (12)

Seasonal Affective Disorder (SAD), occurs during the winter and is caused by a lack of sunlight. A chemical imbalance in the brain takes place and increased levels of the sleep-inducing hormone melatonin are produced. While this is the hormone that induces hibernation in some animals, human symptoms include increased tiredness, lethargy, depression, increased appetite and mood swings.

SAD sufferers can now be treated with light therapy which relieves their symptoms. They need to expose themselves to between two and six hours of very bright light a day. For more help and advice contact your doctor or the SAD ASSOCIATION (refer to Useful contacts).

CHAPTER EIGHT

De-stressing your life

By now you should have realised stress is a very individual thing. What one person finds unbearable and too much, another will thrive on. But no matter what your approach to stress, everyone can benefit from learning how to take the pressure off. So here are 30 ways to de-stress:

30 STRESS BUSTERS

1. Remind yourself you are in control of your life
It sounds ridiculous, but reminding yourself of this can help you stay calm even in the most stressful of situations.

2. Don't be a drama queen
When something stressful happens, tell yourself 'it's not the end of the world!' This will help you to keep things in perspective.

3. Learn to compromise
Accepting that you may not always get everything you want means less stress.

4. Be assertive, not aggressive

There's a big difference between being assertive and being aggressive and yet, people often mix them up. To be assertive you don't have to raise your voice, or be pushy. Learn the difference and your stress levels will reduce.

5. Stand up for yourself

This is an important part of controlling stress. It means learning to not let people manipulate, bully or put you down. If you're not sure how to go about this, try seeking help from people you admire and like. Watch how they handle situations and how they cope with the things you find tricky.

6. Be honest

Especially about how you feel. Learn not to exaggerate the small things such as a disagreement with your best friend or you'll end up blowing them out of all proportion.

7. Say the word 'calm'

Not aloud, but in your head when you're feeling panic ridden or stressed. Repeating the word slowly, over and over, will actually help you to feel calm.

8. Say 'no'

People who can't say no to their friends and family are the ones who are most stressed simply because they give themselves no time or space. Learning how to say no is therefore an excellent way of ensuring you have time to relax.

9. Give yourself more time

Time management is an essential key in the stress game. Before you tackle any big job or work load, work out how you're going to divide your time effectively so you can do all your work, without having to cram.

10. Relax

An obvious one, but do you know how to do it? The key to good relaxation is to do something that takes your mind off everything else. For some people this will be something solitary like going for a walk, for others it will be a night out with friends. Once you've got into a state where you have forgotten all your worries, you can admit to being relaxed.

11. Breathe properly

When we get stressed we forget to breathe properly and start to take fast, shallow breaths, which makes our heart beat faster and oxygen levels fall. When this occurs, signs of stress accelerate in the body. To combat this take deep breaths. For quick fixes at very stressful moments, take three long breaths and then carry on.

12. Count to 10 before you fight back

It's easy to lose control when you're stressed and angry, so make it a rule that you count to 10 (slowly) before you say anything. This will allow you to think before you speak, and help defuse stressful situations.

13. Get organised

One of the main causes of stress is disorganisation. Sort your life out and your stress levels will drop. If you've got a bad memory, write things down. Get into the habit of listing the three things you absolutely have to do each day, so you won't forget.

14. Limit your time worrying

Ever sat down and worried over the same problem for the whole night? If so, think about limiting your worry time. Make it a rule to focus on a problem for only 20 minutes – if after that you've got nowhere, give yourself a break and come back to it later.

15. Do your thinking in the morning

Worrying over your stresses at night is bad news because firstly you're too tired to think properly and secondly, it will stop you from sleeping. Aim to problem solve in the morning when your mind is sharp. If at night you can't sleep, try writing down all your worries (don't re-read what you've written). You'll be amazed at how transferring stresses from your mind to paper will free you up.

16. Take more exercise

Exercise releases the body's natural painkillers – endorphins, which give you a wonderful high and alleviate pent-up frustration and anxiety. Twenty minutes, three times a week will not only keep you fit, but stop you feeling tired and stressed out.

17. Listen when you argue
It sounds bizarre, but none of us listen enough which means most of us always feel misunderstood. So if you can force yourself to listen to the other person when you're having an argument, you'll not only bring calmness and reason to the situation, but also a stronger likelihood of a solution.

18. Sleep healthily
How much sleep do you need? The recommended amount is 8 hours a day. If you get too much or too little, not only are you going to be more sensitive to the effects of stress, but you're also going to feel irritable all day.

19. Eat healthily
Overdose on high sugar foods and junk food, and you'll send your body's sugar levels rocketing. When your sugar levels plummet, so will your mood and your capacity to cope with everyday pressures. So, eat lots of fruit and vegetables to keep your sugar level balanced.

20. Give yourself a 2 minute panic
There are times when you've just got to let loose and panic. If you feel the need, give yourself a two minute limit. Breathe (see stress buster 11) and then tell yourself, 'I can do this, and if I can't it's not the end of the world.'

21. Prepare

What are fears and anxieties really about? Well, simply the unknown and unexpected. How many times have you become worked up about an exam, only to feel relieved once you've turned the paper over and seen the questions? The key to battling with this kind of anxiety is to prepare – for example, study for an exam, read up on a place you might be visiting, or find out about someone you're afraid of meeting.

22. Deal with your hurt feelings

If you feel wronged in some way, then talk to the person concerned. Harbouring hurt only leads to deep resentment, frustration and stress every time you see that person. If you can talk to the person concerned, you can put an end to the problem once and for all.

23. Ask for help

I can't emphasise this one enough. Asking for help whether you are worried, hurt or snowed under is the best way to deal with stress because admitting you can't cope is the first step to coping.

24. Don't take on other people's moods

If someone is grumpy with you or snaps when you ask them something, don't think it's your fault. The fact is they could have had a bad day, they could be feeling ill, or could just be in a bad mood. Remember, just as you have the right to be grumpy so do they.

25. Don't take on other people's problems
We all have friends we love and care about. However, taking on their problems is a bad move because all it does is take the focus off your own life. If you're doing it because you can't say no to them, realise you may be sabotaging your friendship anyway. Remember, listening won't add stress to your life, but living it with them will.

26. Don't worry
Are you someone who always imagines the worst? If so, it might help you to realise that most of our anxieties and fears are in our heads and never actually happen. If you find yourself on a rollercoaster of what ifs, put your life into perspective. Sure these things could happen, but they are not happening right now, so why are you wasting your time on them.

27. Learn to let go
Are you guilty of holding on to things that upset you? If so, you're just adding to the stresses in your life. A good way to let go of your upsets is to close your eyes and imagine tying all your stresses to a balloon string (exam papers, boyfriends or parents). Then let go of the string and watch the balloon float upwards and out of sight, with all your problems attached. It sounds silly, but it works!

28. Keep things in proportion
If you find yourself stressing over something, stop and ask yourself if you've really got things in proportion. Will your world really fall apart if your boyfriend or girlfriend leaves you – of course not! Will your parents really kill you if you fail your GCSEs – of course they won't! Think about what you're saying to yourself and how you might be adding more stress to an already stressful situation.

29. Work out what's important
Sometimes we suffer from stress overload, simply because we put too much on our plates. If you feel you've no time to even think, then take a look at what's on your plate and take off all the unnecessary things. Worrying about the future, regretting the past and imagining you'll never fall in love are all unimportant stresses. Remember, you can't relax if you're worried about these things.

30. Do one thing each day that makes you feel good
Go on, spoil yourself and do something you love each day. The happiness factor aside, doing something pleasurable will not only have huge benefits in decreasing stress in your life, but it will also give you energy, help you to relax and give you some much needed time out from anxiety.

Useful contacts

YOUR DOCTOR

CALM (Campaign Against Living Miserably) –
0800 58 58 58

CHILDLINE – 0800 1111

DEFEAT DEPRESSION CAMPAIGN
17 Belgrave Square
London SW1X 8PG

EATING DISORDERS ASSOCIATION – 01603 765 050
Support for those with eating problems.

MIND (National Association For Mental Health)
Granta House
15-19 Broadway
Stratford
E15 4EQ
Tel: 0345 660163

MIND produce an excellent leaflet on depression with
more contacts (send a stamped addressed envelope with a
postal order for 45p made payable to MIND).

NO PANIC – 01952 590545
Help for people with panic attacks and phobias.

THE PHOBICS SOCIETY
4 Cheltenham Road
Chorlton-cum-Hardy
Manchester M21 1QN.

SAD ASSOCIATION
PO Box 969
London SW7 2PZ.

THE SAMARITANS – 0345 909090

SANELINE – 0345 678000

YOUNG MINDS
102-108 Clerkenwell Road
London EC1M 5SA
020 7336 8445

YOUTH ACCESS
Magazine Business Centre
11 Newarke Street,
Leicester LE1 5SS.

Tel: 0533 558763
For details of local youth counselling groups.

On the web:
www.stress.org.uk
www.howtomanagestress.co.uk
www.managingstress.com (Centre for Stress Management)
www.isma.org.uk (Institute of Stress Management
Association)
www.thesite.org (teen advice site)
www.healthpro.org.uk/heartbeat (health tips from the
National Heart Research Fund
www.mentalhealth.org.uk/peer (Mental Health Foundation
site for teens)

Glossary

CHRONIC WORRIERS
People who worry constantly about everything.

DEPRESSION
When you experience prolonged unhappiness, isolation, helplessness and despair.

HEADACHES
A pain in the head caused by tension in the muscles around your shoulders and neck.

INNER CRITIC
The voice in your head that sabotages your confidence every time you want to try something new, or do something you're scared of.

MIGRAINE
Pounding headaches that can last for hours or even days.

OBSESSIVE COMPULSIVE DISORDERS
A phobia-like condition in which there are frequent repetitive rituals like washing your hands or checking that the doors are locked.

PANIC ATTACKS
When your body exaggerates its response in a stressful situation

PEER PRESSURE
The stress you get from people your own age to act, think and look a certain way.

PHOBIAS
An irrational real fear of an object, animal or sitaution.

PUBERTY
The beginning of sexual maturity.

SEASONAL AFFECTIVE DISORDER (SAD)
A chemical imbalance in the brain takes place and increased levels of the sleep-inducing hormone melatonin are produced.

SELF-ESTEEM
Good opinion of oneself

SELF-HARM
When someone injures themselves on purpose – for example, by scratching or cutting their skin.

STRESS
A physical, emotional or mental pressure.

TRIGGERS
The object, situation or stress that causes a migraine to come on such as cheese, chocolate or oranges.

Index